The Dog Is Dead

LIANA BROOKS

OTHER WORKS

ALL I WANT FOR CHRISTMAS

All I Want For Christmas Is A Reaper
All I Want For Christmas Is A Werewolf

FLEET OF MALIK

Bodies In Motion
Change of Momentum

HEROES AND VILLAINS

Even Villains Fall In Love
Even Villains Go To The Movies
Even Villains Have Interns
Even Villains Play The Hero (books 1 – 3 omnibus)
The Polar Terror

TIME AND SHADOWS

The Day Before
Convergence Point
Decoherence

SHORTER WORKS

Fey Lights
Prime Sensations
Darkness and Good

Find other works by the author at
www.lianabrooks.com

The Dog Is Dead

INKLET #54

LIANA BROOKS

Inkprint PRESS
www.inkprintpress.com

Print ISBN: 978-1-925825-56-5
eBook ISBN: 9781393232391

www.inkprintpress.com

National Library of Australia Cataloguing-in-Publication Data
Brooks, Liana 1982 –
The Dog Is Dead
42 p.
ISBN: 978-1-925825-56-5
Inkprint Press, Canberra, Australia
1. Fiction—Science Fiction—General 2. Fiction—Women
3. Fiction—Short Stories

First Print Edition: March 2021
Cover design © Inkprint Press
Interior art © Amy Laurens

THE DOG IS DEAD

A PALE HALF-MOON HUNG ABOVE THE pine trees as I walked in the noon sun, wishing instead that I could run. It mocked me with the promise of a life I couldn't have, shouldn't want. The wind whispered, stirring the flowers around my feet as they wilted. I was no good at gardening.

I wasn't good at much, actually. But it was no big deal. Maybe a few hundred years ago when humans had eked out a living by growing their own food it would have mattered, but in the modern world where schooling was a matter of tissue programming and roles were chosen for everyone by a government program decades before they were born, being useful wasn't necessary.

The entire purpose of *my* life was to exist. My parents had money, which was nice. It meant they could afford to own land here on Earth and buy me a modest education when I turned ten: three hours of reading, writing, and basic mathematics programmed straight into my cerebrum.

When I was fifteen, my parents bought me a secondary education, allowing me to discuss classic literature with everyone else in my social strata. We'd all been programmed with the same six lectures, so our conversations usually devolved into recitations, seeing who could remember them best.

At eighteen I was tested, found intelligent enough to receive a basic civilian file (programmed into my head in fifteen minutes), and shunted into Slot 37B-12D5: housewife.

If my parents had been poor, we would have been relocated to Prima, the main lunar base that hung like a golden star over the moon's surface.

If they'd been wealthier, I would have received a fuller education that prepared me for more than balancing a check book.

If I'd been more intelligent, I would have earned a place among the scientists who filled Stellar base on the far side of the moon, the ones who'd be first chosen for any new colonies in the stars beyond.

In the secret watches of the night, when I stepped away from my cold bed to gaze at the stars, that's what I wished for.

Something new. A glimmer of opportunity to be someone else. To remove the choking grip of societal norms and replace it with the heady sensation of not knowing what would happen next.

But here, in the noon light, under a half moon white as the clouds, I knew I would never have those things. I knew it as a child, and I would remain faithful to that truth until the day I turned ninety-seven and reported to the hospital to be humanely put down, sure in the knowledge that some young girl would arrive at my house the next morning to wear my clothes and walk my dog, because that is what Citizen 37B-12D5 does three times a day, rain or shine.

Of course, it wasn't a real dog, which would be cruel. It was a Canine Companion with FeelReal-Furr and a life-like bark. None of my schooling included information on dogs, so I had no words to describe it...

Him... Her... It.

That bothered me.

I wished I knew what words to say if I ever brought my pet up in conversation, but I didn't. I never would.

It was black. It came to my knee. It was programmed to need five kilometers of walking every day, which ensured I received the necessary exercise for my age and metabolism. With one last wistful glance at the moon, I checked the mail (nothing) and returned to the house.

As I did every day, I watered a bowl of dead petunias on the front step, swept the wooden floors, and checked that the computer had ordered dinner for us.

We were having pot roast. Everyone on the block was having pot roast. As far as I knew, everyone in my social strata was eating pot roast tonight. With slightly overcooked carrots and a choice of water or apple juice to drink.

I didn't want pot roast. I didn't want to water petunias. I didn't want to wait for another hour until my lawfully wedded husband arrived home from his government job to eat dinner.

I went to the door, twisting the handle, even though I knew it was futile.

A melodic chime signaled the end of my momentary rebellion. "This door is locked for your security. Please state the reason you wish this door opened at this time."

"I want to go outside." My hand dropped to my side. I knew it was fruitless. It wasn't in the script. Citizen B37-12D5 never went outside in the afternoon.

"Did you forget to check the mail?" the computer asked.

"No."

"Would you like to watch some television?" Unbidden, the television in the corner turned on, showing a comedy about life in the corporate world. "Your friends and neighbours all enjoy this show. Why not join them in a light-hearted laugh as Randi and Co. try to make Mister Meeker forget his glasses?"

"I don't wish to watch television. I want to go outside."

"Perhaps you would like to call a friend?" the computer suggested.

"I would like to go outside."

"Why don't you log in to your social network and plan a picnic? Everyone loves picnics." A screen on the kitchen table shimmered to life and showed a running stream of the thoughts of my 'friends'. They were all very similar; we did all have the same twenty-thousand-word vocabulary after all.

"Thank you," I lied to the computer. "That sounds very engaging."

I sat down and watched as people typed the lines from the show as it played behind me in the living room. As Mister Meeker outsmarted Randi and Co. once again, a gray car drove up to our house. My husband exited it, checked his tie, locked the door, and counted forty-eight steps precisely.

The door unlocked for him and he stepped inside. "Hello, dear. You look well. Did you have a good walk with the dog?"

"Yes." The word was past my lips before I even considered another option. "Dinner is ready."

"Good. I had a busy day. I'm hungry."

I mouthed the words with him. In four years living together, our conversation never varied. Sometimes I wondered if he was as robotic as the canine companion now lying inactive by the fake fireplace. "What would you like to drink?"

"Water, please."

I stood, and again rebellion flared. I arranged our dinner plates and gave us both apple juice. Instead of taking the eight carrots allotted to me, I piled all sixteen carrots on his plate and took both slices of meat. "Dinner is ready."

My husband took off his tie and looked at our plates. "D... d... d..."

"Your line is, 'Dinner looks delicious.'" I folded my napkin on my lap and waited for him to sit.

After a moment he sat beside me. "Dinner looks different."

"I tried something new today. You will like it."

I hoped I was lying. I hoped he hated it. I hoped he threw his plate and broke a window so I could run out through the glass and watch the moon set in the darkness.

He ate his carrots. "Dinner was delicious. Thank you."

And it was over.

Now he would go to shower, change into a bathrobe, and watch two hours and thirty-one minutes of television before yawning once and going to bed.

I sat at the table staring at the two slices of meat on my plate.

I was only hurting myself by not eating. No one else would notice. No one else would care. And if by some small chance I was able to resist food for days on end until I made myself sick, I would only be transferred to the hospital and be reprogrammed. Or put down.

I dumped the meat on the canine companion's food bowl, on top of the fake kibble I put in for verisimilitude. The canine companion could only eat on command and I'd never ordered it to eat before. Now I did. "Dog. Eat."

Wagging its tail, the robotic construct chewed on the real meat—and choked. Its eyes sizzled for a moment, flashing red, and then it fell over with a hollow clang.

My husband laughed at something on the television.

I walked over, standing in front of the screen so I could block his view.

"The dog is dead."

My husband struggled. This wasn't part of the script. This is not what we did every day. This was new.

I nearly clapped with joy. This was new! I didn't know his answer! I didn't know what came next!

"Why is the dog dead?"

"The dog ate food. The dog choked. The dog is dead."

My husband stood up and turned to look at the canine companion. "Dogs should not eat people food." He sat back down and laughed even though the television was showing a commercial for toothpaste.

Everyone loved that commercial. When I ordered groceries online on Tuesdays, the screen always told me it was the one my friends liked.

I wondered about that. Was there any other kind of toothpaste?

If I wanted to buy something that none of my friends had tried, would the computer let me? Would I like it if I did?

There was no way of knowing. I sat beside the dead dog. My husband watched his television shows and went to bed. The lights in the house turned off. The steady hum of electronics died as the computer decided we were asleep.

Why it followed his schedule and not mine, I wasn't sure. The computer would remind my husband to go to bed, but never me. Once he was home and I was safely locked inside, nothing else seemed to matter. Proof that the computer was just as dumb as everyone else.

I watched the moon set, Prima shining like a gem.

Was there someone out there who wanted to be me? Did that person have a number like I did, a place in society like mine? Or did they have a name?

I showered after the moon set, got dressed, and lay in bed waiting for sleep to come. It never did. I wasn't tired. I was bored. I wanted...

Something. I wanted to go outside.

When my husband woke up early, I picked up the dog and followed him to the door. This wasn't in the script. Fear filled his eyes.

"I'm putting the dog outside."

"I think the dog wants a walk." When in doubt, stick to the script.

We both looked at the spot where the canine companion should have been jumping with its tongue hanging out.

"Yes. I guess I should walk the dog."

He nodded. "Have a good day."

As the door closed, I shoved the dog's body in the way. The lock clicked shut and the television turned on the morning news.

I stepped outside as the reporter detailed what a beautiful morning drive it was today.

Canine companions couldn't walk on grass, so we always followed the sidewalk on a loop through the neighborhood, screened by pine trees. On the way I'd see glimpses of the highway in the distance. At one point, you could even see the spires of the city buildings. I didn't know which city; geography cost extra.

This morning I walked on the grass, watching it bend under my heavy tread. Each step smothered to death countless plant cells.

I was incautious.

Uncaring.

I reveled in their tragic demise.

I twisted the toe of my shoe into the turf, relishing the feel of grass dying under foot. I imagined little screams of plant terror echoing to the cold stars above. I imagined the gasp of shock and denial as someone from Prima looked down and saw me savagely destroying a plant they could never touch because they were banished from the very planet of their birth.

The sweet scent of cut grass invigorated me. I ran.

Over the lawns and past the pines I ran, to the edge of the highway where auto-piloted cars flew past, their passage whipping my hair up. My heart raced as I realized I could end it all here. None of those cars could stop. None of the drivers even knew how to.

I could leap and after a moment of blinding pain, everything would be over.

I jumped.

The cars stopped.

They hung in the air like frozen hummingbirds, unreal.

Tentatively, I reached out a hand to touch a bright red cruiser. The car was hot. The driver inside looked back at me, confused, uncertain. We were off script. Off the script. Off the page. Off the writing desk and floundering.

I stepped through the space between cars. Skipping, dancing. They moved around, resumed their flow. Everything was as it should be except that here and there—wherever I stepped—they froze. I was the queen of chaos, suspending the birds in their flight.

Life happened around me as I wandered down the lines of the highway. People went to work. One car I stopped had an old man with a dark face, somber and sad. I knew without a word that he was on his way to the hospital to die. I stepped away and his car moved on, rolling with the tide of humanity to its destination, inevitable, unavoidable.

Inescapable.

I followed. It was that or find my way back to the pine trees and the

quiet suburban house where my canine companion lay dead.

If I went back, the doors would lock.

If the doors locked, I'd never escape
again.

If I never ran, I'd never know how
far I could go.

THE MAKING OF
THE DOG IS DEAD

In fall of 2011, I moved to the most beautiful hell on Earth. It was an idyllic, rambling farm house on three acres in the panhandle of Florida. We had woods on either side, a large pasture, a barn, quirky little doors leading to hidden rooms...

At night, I could walk outside and see the Milky Way. During the day, the air was scented by gardenia and magnolias. My children ran free, plucking blackberries from the wild bushes and playing on the swing set while the dog watched.

It was warm and perfect and I was so miserable that it seemed like torture.

In the beautiful setting, where everything was fine, I was struggling with severe postpartum depression. Every day was the same brutal routine of caring for a colicky infant, seeing the older children off, and waiting for my husband to come home from a job that had him traveling for weeks at a time. Inside my head there was unending turmoil and chaos. But, from the outside, we looked so happy. The perfect little family.

My neighbours never guessed anything was amiss.

I had no friends nearby and I felt caged in a gilded prison. I wrote this piece as an escape. I wrote the perfect world of my cage for everyone to see, and then I broke it.

A few months later we moved again, this time to a duplex with no noticeable backyard. My neighbor was a concert-trained pianist who played concertos every afternoon at four and I was never so grateful for a shared wall as I was for that one.

Read more by Liana Brooks!

FEY LIGHTS

Dark water writhed over the ship's deck, a living thing hunting for prey, stinging like acid where it touched bare skin. Jeani stumbled over the guts of her ship, swearing in every language she knew. Her foot fell through a hole in the deck created by the crash. Hot metal gouged her leg as tears ran down her cheeks.

I don't want to die like this. There has to be a way out.

There is a way out. The same way the water is coming in.

Running was out of the question. Half-limping, half-swimming through the rising water, Jeani forced herself back to the rear of the ship, navigating by touch and the weak glow of the emergency lights that hadn't burst, back to the gaping wound that was once the engine room and secondary hold. Pressure from the rapid descent into the gravity well and the gushing water warped the frame, creating a strong current. Jeani grabbed the free-fall handle near the emergency door and pressed her free hand to the glowing lock.

Nothing.

She tried yanking the override.

Nothing.

She kicked the door with her good leg.

Pressure sent the door flying inwards at the head of a tidal wave. Jeani gasped for air and went under. Seconds ticked away as she grappled blindly for the next free-fall handle, the current tugging at her.

The hand-hold slipped out of her grip. She pushed up once, bumping her head against the high ceiling of the engine room as she gasped for air. The current swirled under her, pulling her down into the darkness.

Saltwater stung her face. She shuddered as something nipped at her bleeding leg. Ignoring the pain, she clawed at the water until she broke through and gasped in the alien atmosphere. Water crashed over her in the darkness.

Rough, warm sand rubbed against her skin. Sucking in a lungful of the oxygen-rich air, Jeani flipped onto her stomach and pulled herself away from the water. It lapped at her legs, a wayward lover begging her to return.

She laughed as she looked at the strange stars overhead. Her lungs burned, her leg ached, she was shaking with delayed shock, but she was alive. "See, Hothi, I told you I wasn't going to die that easy."

Dominique pushed through the crowd and looked down at the beach.

"Could be a Lander," Gregor said as he adjusted his cap. "Saw the prison ships sailing past this last moon. Could be a Lander," he repeated with a final snort.

A knife waved past Dominique's face, stabbing toward the figure on the beach. "'Twere wedding lights last night. Lit up the sky with fire, set the trees to burning," said Beau.

"'Tain't no fire touched the trees. Trees are fine," Gregor argued. "'Tis a Lander."

"Fey fire," someone said behind him. "Fey burn things with cold fire." A fist hit Dominique's shoulder. "Fey can turn a man's bones to ice. They summon monsters from the deep."

One of the women crossed her fingers and made the sign of the arch to ward off the ill will of the deep dwellers.

"Landers bring plague," Adrian said grimly. He too tapped Dominique's shoulder. "We can't let a Lander near the village."

"We's best shooting it from here," Gregor said.

Another shook his head. "Arrows can't touch fey."

"You volunteering to go down there to slit its throat?" Gregor demanded.

"Such a thing to ask a man! I've got kin, I have."

There was the sound of shuffling feet. A cool sea breeze wrapped around Dominique's legs as the crowd parted. He filled their silence with imagined conversations.

"He's a Lander," one would say in the Silent way of the island-born. *"Got no kin nor woman of his own, does he,"* someone else would murmur.

Dominique kept the snarl he felt forming in his throat from escaping.

"Will you go?" Adrian whispered, confirming his suspicions. "None will make you, if you say no."

"You'll go?" Dominique asked with a half-smile. Adrian wasn't a bad man. Island born, birthed in the sea, born running on the beach and listening to the waves.

The island-born claimed the waves spoke back to those that listened. The saltwater seeped into their blood so they could hear the thoughts of others like they heard the song of the ocean. Like all the island born, Adrian had no trouble believing every infamy laid against the Landers who lived on the far side of the ocean, in the land of the tyrant.

Adrian shrugged. "Better to slit the Lander's throat on the beach than let it breathe on a child in the village. We'll all die of black blood and fever before the tide is high."

"I'll go," Dominique said, loud enough for his voice to carry to the back of the crowd. "I'll go see to the Lander. I'll send him down to the docks in the south. He can find work there if he likes."

"What if it be fey?" Gregor asked, eyes wide.

Dominique studied the lone figure on the distant sand below, a sad creature sprawled under the hot morning sun. "The fey have a treaty with the Tyrant of Urull. The first tyrant traded his soul for the secrets of the fey lights—wedding lights," he corrected himself, using the island-born term. "The first tyrant lost his mind when the fey showed him the wonders of their world. Men that could turn into dogs. Deep monsters that could walk as men. Women so beautiful that they could suck the soul of a man as he walked past, steal his life with a kiss.

"The tyrants all have made a pact

with the fey, traded their subjects to the fey for their favor, but they've never let the fey roam the lands. No fey walk outside the tyrant's gates in Urull. No fey step on the white sands of the islands."

"Maybe this one is outcast," Beau said. "A prisoner, like all the other Landers sent here."

"You've got a leak in your hull," Adrian said, punching Beau in the arm. "You think the tyrant could make a prisoner out of the fey? You think a man could keep one of them under lock and key?"

"But... wedding lights!" Beau lookeded to Dominique for support. "The lights haven't touched our sky in years."

"No one's been out walking in years," Dominique said. "Who was out last night?" He turned and scanned the crowd.

Hardy folk, the island-born. They

wore homespun cloth, britches of old sail cloth traded from down the coast, filigree gold necklaces twined around shells and sea gems. All of them came from Lander families at some point in their history, Landers who had either escaped the tyrants, or been banished to a slow death on the distant islands, depending on who you asked.

But the islands were in their blood now. They spoke in Silence, and left him an outcast. The women looked away from him, the older men met his gaze, and one boy blushed. "Tris? Were you out walking last night?"

The boy with dark eyes and a thatch of red hair looked up. "May have been. What's it to you?"

Someone chuckled.

"Explains the wedding lights," Gregor muttered. "You still ought to slit the throat first. That one's not going to give you any answer you'll be wanting."

Keep reading! Head to
**www.inkprintpress.com/
lianabrooks/feylights/**
to buy your copy now!

ABOUT THE AUTHOR

Liana Brooks loves big dogs, cheerful children, and a job that allows her to be home more often than not. When she isn't traveling, she enjoys writing science fiction in every form, from sprawling space operas romances (the *Fleet of Malik* series, starting with *Bodies In Motion*), to the antics of a superpowered family (the *Heroes and Villains* series, which can be read in any order), to intricate time-travel murder mysteries (the *Time And Shadow* series, starting with *The Day Before*).

Liana also maintains a soft spot for paranormal romances. She writes the popular *All I Want For Christmas* novellas, including *All I Want For Christmas Is A Werewolf* and *All I Want For Christmas Is A Reaper*.

You can learn more about her and her books at www.LianaBrooks.com

INKLETS

Collect them all! Released on the 1st and 15th
of each month.

INKLET #055
Allure
AMY LAURENS

The LIES we KNOW
LIANA BROOKS

AFTERMATH & Fool Me Once
AMY LAURENS
INKLET #057

INKLET #058
Purity
An Age Of Unicorns Story
AMY LAURENS

INKLET #059
Saved
AMY LAURENS

INKLET #060
A Kiss is the Secret
AMY LAURENS

INKLET #061
A Changing Tides Story
Fire Bright
AMY LAURENS

INKLET #062
Hades AND Persephone
LIANA BROOKS

INKLET #063
Just So Long As You're Happy
AMY LAURENS

INKLET #064
Theft Of A Lifetime
LIANA BROOKS

INKLET #065
Shoe
AMY LAURENS

INKLET #066
Published AUTHOR
LIANA BROOKS

DOUBLE ISSUE
INKLET #067
THE REMARKABLE INSIGHT OF JELLYBEANS & Understanding
AMY LAURENS

INKLET #068
Desperate Measures
AMY LAURENS

INKLET #069
Rock-a-bye
LIANA BROOKS

INKLET #070
the Other Carly
AMY LAURENS

INKLET #071
Bs By Bioluminescent light
AMY LAURENS

INKLET #072
Even Villains Grant Wishes
A Heroes & Villains Story
LIANA BROOKS

www.ingramcontent.com/pod-product-compliance
Lightning Source LLC
Chambersburg PA
CBHW032053180726
48284CB00004B/1322